BOOK ONE

HOUSE OF MIRRORS

A Cheap Chills Thriller

BY
K. N. BUCK

HOSTED BY
PROF. T. LEEZARD

Airleaf
Publishing

airleaf.com

ISBN: 1-59453-901-4

To my wife Brenda, who has faith in me always.
I pledge my love to you.

Dreams, fears and desires.
All of us have these same traits.
For most of us, we dream that our desires will come true.
And then there are those that FEAR that they will.

K. N. BUCK

ACKNOWLEDGMENTS

I would like to thank the following people:
Brenda for her encouragement and support.
Miss O'hara and Miss Titus my seventh grade English
teachers.
NOVA DEVELOPMENT for the inside illustrations.
My mom and dad for letting me stay up late to watch Alfred
Hitchcock Presents.
And to all the little people along the way, you know who you
are.

TABLE OF CONTENTS

* INTRO *

"Step right up. Don't be shy. The show is about to begin. Right this way, right this way. Have your tickets ready. Let me introduce myself. My name is Proffesor T. LeeZard. You may call me Proffessor T. LeeZard. I don't know you well enough yet, for you to call me by my first name. That will be my little secret, at least for a little while. With the aid of my magical walking cane, whom I call Dragon stick, I will be your host, your guide and your head cook, serving up a main course of chills with a side order of screams and nightmares. If you were looking for a good book to help you sleep, this isn't the one. If you scare easy, put it down, now! But, if your looking for something to get your heart and mind racing, go ahead and read this book. And now, with a wave of my Dragon stick. Step right up, step right up, the story is about to begin. It's all here, on the inside."

Proffessor T. LeeZard

"The Carnival Midway"

PROLOGUE

(**prologue** n. an introduction to play, poem, story, etc., fore-
shadows future event.)

The not too distant future.

It's an early June night in Indiana. The scene is of a
Midwest County Fair, viewed from above. A steady stream of
cars flow into a grass field and park in row after row. Young
and old, stroll through the entrance. As the view widens to the
whole panorama, all of the sights and sounds associated with
the fair stab at the senses. The Ferris Wheel and Roller Coaster
are visible in the night sky as giant metal sculptures of light.
Bright lights sparkle and blink as rides whirl and pulse in time
with the ever-present heavy music.

Coming in closer through the Midway, there are lines of
anxious riders waiting to be next. Handing over their tightly
clutched ticket for the chance to be thrilled.

Next on the Midway are all of the sideshows and games.
Colorful awnings decorate the front of each booth, with every

stuffed animal imaginable peeking out from under. The row of game booths gives way to all of the sideshow attractions, with all of their outlandish banners on display. Signs and banners advertising such wonders as The Snake Woman, The Rubber Man, The Sword Swallower and such. In front of each sideshow booth stands a small crowd; their attention transfixed on every word that the man at the front of the tent has to offer.

One of those sideshow barkers. A ragged dressed, toothless fellow, he is trying to coax passers-by to come in and see his featured freak.

"Come on, hey you! Over here. Yea you," yelling as he motions to a group of freewheeling youths. They walk on and ignore his taunts.

"What? Scared to come in?" He shouts as he spits a stream of tobacco juice between his teethe and words and wiping his chin.

"Come on, come in and show your friends that you've got some balls." The youths walk on without giving in to his appeal. Moving away, on down the row of booths.

The man continues in the background, "Come in and see ZAMBORA, half woman, half ape. Caged, alive inside. Is she real? Take the dare. Zambora caged…" his voice fading in the distance, drowned out by all the other sounds of the midway.

"Is she ape or woman…"

A slightly diabolic looking clown wonders through the crowd. He grins wildly at everyone. He seems to frighten the children; more then making them laugh. The clown turns and walks on through the crowd.

"Mommy look! Look at the funny boy." A small boy of six or seven stands memorized, looking into the warped reflection in a Fun House Mirror. The mirror sits just outside the entrance to the HOUSE OF MIRRORS.

"He's all crooked. He's waving his hands at me." The boy continues to giggle at the twisted shapes he sees in the mirror.

The boy's mother, a young professional looking woman, stands off to the side, talking on her cell phone. She is oblivious to her child. Finishing her call, she sharply looks around for her son. She walks over to his side and takes his hand.

"Come on. We're going to be late, if you don't stop wondering off." She pulls him away from the mirror. He wants to stay there a little longer. He can hardly be pulled from his place. His gaze impaled to the reflection.

"Now that's enough. We have to go." She pays very little attention to the mirror.

"Oh! Let him look. Let him go inside." The voice comes from an old woman. She is sitting at the entrance to the House of Mirrors. Her face is old and stained with life. She wears too much lipstick and her eyebrows seem to be painted on. A faded red ribbon, a bit tattered, holds back a mass of hair that perhaps was once blond, but now is mostly grey.

"He's having so much fun. You should let him go inside." The gravel-voiced woman continues, "The WONDERS are inside."

"No." The boy's mother responds.

"We're running late now."

"No, please—you must let him see the COLLECTION of mirrors, on the inside. You can wait here if you want—I'll even let him go in for free."

The boy's mother grabs her child's hand.

"Let's go, come on!"

She pulls the boy away and they head off at a hurried pace. She turns and glances back over her shoulder at the old woman. She clutches her son closer as they disappear into the crowd.

The look of disappointment is evident on the old woman's face. Getting off of her stool. She slowly walks over to the mirror standing by the entrance. The woman takes out a silk hanky and wipes at the mirror ever so lovingly. She looks into it, at the blurry image of a small boy. He is visibly weeping in the depths of the silvery reflection.

"Maybe—next time. Maybe next time, I can. Maybe next time," she seems to be consoling the figure in the mirror. She wistfully brushes her hand across the surface.

"Please don't cry. Maybe next time, I can get you a companion." She strokes her fingers over the cold glass once more.

"The Boskowitz Home"

* CHAPTER ONE *

October 1957
Thursday.

It's evening. The wind and light drizzle of rain beat a steady rhythm, splashing on piles of raked leaves along the curb. The leaves swirl and blow up to the front of an old Victorian house, one along a row of such houses. The leaves land at the welcome mat in front of the large oak door. To the left of the door sits a Halloween jack-o-lantern. The brass address plate on the door reads 19080 Deedmoore TR.

The house has a real Leave It to Beaver atmosphere about it. Inside, a television plays in the background.

"Carpet as low as four ninety five a square yard. Call now," comes the voice from a commercial.

A clever jingle plays and the announcer gives the phone number.

"Five eight, eight, four, three hundred. Call now."

The house is very cozy. Sounds of dinner being prepared waft in from the kitchen. A plush carpeted flight of stairs, is the main focal point at the center of the house. At the top of these stairs is Steven's room.

The room is too small, for all of the coveted collectibles that line every inch of free space.

Steven is a shy boy. At fifteen, most boys this age, would be out-going and busy doing teenage boy stuff. Steven, on the other hand, could most likely be found at home. Alone in his room, locked away in there.

Steven is a collector. A collector of anything that he felt was special. To someone else, these things might seem worthless or a waste of time. But not, to Steven. All of these things were priceless. They were all treasures. Bug collections, rocks, his coveted comic book collection, and of course his baseball cards. He spent many hours here, lost with his treasures.

The telephone rings downstairs.

"Hello! Boskowitz residence." Steven's mom cradles the phone under her chin as she speaks.

"Oh hello Tommy. Hold on, he's upstairs in his room. I'll get him."

She turns and yells up to Steven. "Steven, pick up the telephone. It's Tommy."

"He should be right with you Tommy. Hold on." She puts the phone down, tightens up her apron string and returns to the kitchen.

Upstairs, in Steven's room. Steven sits on the edge of his bed. He leans over on one elbow and continues sorting through some baseball cards. He's lost in his own little world. As the door is shut, Steven did not hear his mothers call.

Steven's mother returns to the downstairs phone, aware that Steven still hasn't picked up the telephone extension.

"I'm sorry Tommy. He must not of heard me call him. Tell you what, I'm about to set dinner on the table, so after we eat, I'll make sure to have Steven call you back. Is that Ok?"

"Sure thing Mrs. B. That'll be fine. Thanks."

"Ok then, Bye now." She hangs up the phone and goes back to attend to dinner.

Later that evening, Steven has finished all of his after dinner chores and heads back to his room to return Tommy's call.

Tommy is one of Steven's best friends from school. Tommy Toth, he hated being called Tommy now that he was a teenager. Steven and Tom made up two parts of a threesome. The third member was Kevin Shea. Kevin was the wild one of the three, always finding some kind of trouble to lead them all into. Tom is more of a follower, than a leader. There were times in the past when the boys were inseparable. Where you found one, the others would surely be close behind.

Now that they were getting older, they seemed to be spending less and less time together. Tommy and Kevin have found other friends and new interests at school. Interests, that didn't seem to include Steven. Occasionally, Tom would call and invite Steven to join him and Kevin for a movie at the mall in Concord. Steven always felt like a fifth wheel in these circumstances. Both Kevin and Tom would have their girl friends with them. So it was always best that Steven decline the invitation. In the last year or so, Kevin and Steven have had a few big arguments. Kevin wasn't as nice to Steven as he once was. He never seemed to miss a chance at putting Steven down in front of everyone.

Steven, prepared to turn down yet another invitation from Tommy, he picks up the phone and dials. He waits for Tom to answer. Steven occupies his ideal hand by leafing through an old copy of Action Comics.

"Hey." Tommy answers. Trying to sound cool.

"Hey," responds Steven, with the same attempt at cool.

"Ya know, I hate it when your mom calls me Tommy. We're not little kids anymore, ya know?"

"I know what you mean. She thinks I'm still her little man." Steven responds.

"Well you are kind of short." Tom tries to be smart. He makes only himself laugh. He almost chokes on the fist full of potato chips that he has crammed into his mouth. He spits excess crumbs to the floor as he continues to catch his breath.

"God, Tom, you're such an idiot sometimes. So, what's up?

"I was just calling to…" He stops and burps into the phone. "…To see what time you want to meet on Saturday…or have you forgotten?"

"Forgotten what?" Steven asks, with an unseen grin.

"Kevin's party, you turd," still munching into the phone.

"Oh yeah, I forgot. Hey, what are you going to dress as this Halloween?"

This was Steven's favorite time of year. October, when leaves turn gold and fall to the ground, cooler breezes replace those of gentle warmth. Kevin's annual Halloween party was always one of the highlights of the season. Every year since Kevin's family had moved here, they always had the very best Halloween parties.

Tommy speaks up, "I thought that you knew. I thought that you knew, Kevin changed his mind, he's not having a costume party."

"Why not? I thought since his parents were going to be away...That he was set on having it."

"No, he's still having it, only...only." Tom begins to grin into the phone. "Only, this year he invited girls to the party. You know what a football stud Kevin thinks he is. Besides, dressing up is a bit childish. Don't you think?"

Steven pulls nervously on the phone cord. Twisting it into a tangle of wire.

"Steve, ya know whose going to be there?" Tommy asks, in a lowered voice.

Steven says nothing. He shakes his head to himself. He is not thrilled with the thought of girls being there. He never knew what to say or how to act in their company. He, no doubt, would end up sitting quietly alone, off in some little corner or perhaps a completely different part of the house.

Kevin was the popular one of the three, especially with the girls. He was on the football team and the track team. Tommy did all right for himself with the girls. Steven just didn't have the nerve to talk to them. Steven did have an interest in one girl though.

"Hey, Steve, ya know who's going to be there?" Tom asks a second time, with a smile in his voice.

"Sarah Trottier," blurts Tommy, not waiting for Steven's reply.

That was she. The one girl that Steven had a bit of a crush on. Sarah Trottier.

"Sarah? Are you sure?" Steven's voice is now a little excited. "Are you sure?"

"Absolutely. Sarah is in charge of all the entertainment for the party. Why? Does that bother you? I thought that you kind of liked her. Besides, she has the hots for you, ya know."

Steven pauses. He does like Sarah. He nervously shuffles his feet and then changes the subject.

"Tom, what time are we supposed to be at Kevin's house on Saturday?"

"I'll come over to your house around seven. We can walk over to Kevin's from there. Ok?"

"Yea. Yea, I guess that will be Ok." Steven is both scared and excited. "I have to get going now. I'll talk to you tomorrow at school. Later."

"Yea, later Steve."

Steven hangs up the receiver and sits further back on his bed. He picks up a pile of rare comic books that he had been looking through. One by one he reorganizes them and gently puts them back into their protective bags. He gets up and stores his collection of comics in the closet. Flopping back down on the bed, Steven can't help thinking about Sarah Trottier.

"It's morning in the Boskowitz house."

* CHAPTER TWO *

October 1957
Friday.

It's morning in the Boskowitz house. The sun is streaming in through the kitchen window, as Steven's mom is busy preparing pancakes and sliced fruit at the counter. Steven wonders into the kitchen and plops himself down at the table. His mom brings over a large bowl of fruit. She arranges a plate and places it in front of Steven. Steven is not very interested in eating this morning. He is preoccupied in thought.

"So, are you getting excited about Kevin's party this weekend?" Steve's mom asks as she sits down at the table with Steven.

"I guess so. But…"

"What is it Hun?" Sensing that her son is troubled with something, she puts her hand on his.

"I don't know." Steven fumbles.

"It's ok Steven. You can tell your old mom," she laughs trying to get a smile out of Steven. "Besides, your dad is already gone for work. It's just you and me kid. You can tell me anything. Don't you know that?"

Steven begins picking at the fruit in his bowl. Nervously pushing each piece from one side of the dish to the other.

"Well, it's like this," he begins. "You know how every year Kevin has his Halloween party?"

"Yes I know. Go on," she prods Steven.

"Well, this year, it's not going to be just us guys there. Kevin decided to make it a boy girl party, instead. Sarah Trottier is going to be there. You know that girl that I told you about. She is in charge of all the entertainment and games at the party."

"So, what is exactly your problem with that? I thought that you kind of liked Sarah. Don't you?"

"Yea." Steven replies sheepishly. He does like Sarah. They sit together in several classes at school. And unbeknownst to his two friends, Tommy and Kevin, Steven and Sarah had met at the library several times to study together. On those occasions, Steven would be deep in study and Sarah would always tease him trying to get him to loosen up. She made Steven laugh. Yes, he liked her all right.

"It's not that I have a problem with Sarah. It's the way Tommy and Kevin tease me about her, Just because she acts and dresses a little different. Not so much Tommy, mostly, it's Kevin. He's not the same as he used to be. It's like they put her in charge of the party games and stuff because they wanted to make fun of her or something."

"Steven, didn't you tell me, that her family just moved here?"

"Yea, they came from some country in Europe. I think Sarah told me that her family was in the Entertainment industry and that they move all around. She said that they were from Moldavia or something like that. Sarah has a bit of an accent that is barely noticeable."

"Well that's no reason to make fun of people. I'm sure that every thing will be just fine," she pats Steven's hand. "Don't you worry about it." She thinks that it's cute that her son has a girlfriend.

"You better get going sweetie. You don't want to be late for school."

Steven hurries to eat a few pieces of fruit. He jumps up and grabs the sack lunch from the counter. Peanut butter and jelly with a banana, his favorite. Steven leans over and kisses his mother on the cheek as he runs past her.

"Thanks mom." And out the door he goes.

Whitman Junior High School.

"Though built of brick and stone, those that enter, take wisdom home"

* CHAPTER THREE *

Whitman Junior High School.

There's a chill in the morning air and a kind of crispness that makes one feel, alive. Steven walks the same path to school every day. Taking the same short cut through back alleys and back yards. It is no coincident, that Steven's short cut to school takes him down the very street where Sarah lives.

The Trottier house sits up on a hill. It's over grown shrubbery and rusted iron fences had seen better days. Sarah's father, obviously, was not the work around the house type. She had told Steven that her father was gone quite a bit. The house had been the target of pranksters on several occasions. Eggs, toilet paper and leaves had at one time or another, been deposited on the house and property. The house did have a foreboding look about it. Although Sarah had asked Steven on several occasions to come over and study, Steven had always felt it better to study together at the library.

It was about a mile walk from Steven's house to the school. On a good day, he could make the trip in about eight minutes. This was one of those good days. Steven made it in record time. As Steven approaches the old stone arch in front of the school, he reads a little brass sign. A little sign that no one pays much attention to.

"Though built of brick and stone, those that enter, take wisdom home." Steven reads the words out loud. As he nears the steps to the school, he sees Tommy leaning against the outside wall. Other students rush up the steps on their way to class, practically knocking Steven to the ground. He notices that Tommy is wearing a black, leather motorcycle jacket. A jacket that looks like it might take Tom a few years to grow into. He's eating something as usual.

"Nice jacket man." Steven says as he approaches. "Where'd ya get it? Is it real leather? Holy cow, my mom would kill me if she caught me wearing something like that to school."

"My mom doesn't know that my brother gave it to me when he left for the navy. I hide it in the shed, out back of the house. That way, I can grab it when I leave in the morning.

"It's really cool, Tom."

Tommy takes the last bite of his Baby Ruth. Now as he continues to act the part of cool, he takes a comb from his back pocket and begins to groom his hair back.

"You see Kevin yet this morning?" Tom asks.

Before Steven can answer, Tommy motions to a crowd of girls. Kevin is in the center of the crowd. Truly the big man on campus. Kevin tosses a football from hand to hand as he talks to girls. He looks over at Steven and Tom. He barely acknowledges them with a nod. The group breaks up, a few girls are left standing by the drinking fountain.

"Sarah's over there Steve. You gonna go talk to her? Or do you want me to talk to her for ya?" Tom can't help trying to egg Steven on.

"I might," counters Steven.

Tommy shrugs his shoulders at Steven and then heads off to catch up to Kevin.

Steven goes over to the drinking fountain. Sarah is standing alone now. She watches Steven, as he makes his way toward her. She smiles at him. Steven looks down at his feet, to shy to smile.

Sarah is a plain looking girl. She is both a little older and taller than Steven is. Her clothes always look a bit out of place and style. This morning she was wearing her usual, a pink smock dress with a red striped apron. She wore a red ribbon in her blond hair. Plain looking or not, Steven thought that she was special.

Steven walks up to Sarah. "Hi there."

"Hi Steve. So, was Tommy giving you a hard time this morning?"

"Just a little," says Steven. "He was razzing me about you."

"Oh, he'll get over it. Both, Tommy and Kevin need to grow up. Don't let them get to you. Ok?"

"I know." Steven feels better now. "Guess I'll see you at Kevin's party this Saturday."

"Yea, I'm planning some really scary games for everyone. It will be something that they won't forget anytime soon. It'll be a blast. And besides, we can spend some time together."

Sarah moves in closer to Steven, "You know…I've been wanting to talk to about something."

The school bell rings at that very moment. Students go darting past Steven and Sarah. Sarah leans closer to Steven and kisses him on the cheek.

"Better go. We can't be late for first hour class. Maybe we can talk later, in Mr. Black's science class." Sarah rubs Steven's hand. "I want you to be with me forever."

Steven says nothing. He just smiles at Sarah. He's not really sure how to take that last statement. They head off up the steps and down the hall in separate directions.

Later that same day, as third hour science class begins, all of the students are busy setting up for the days lecture and experiments. Sinks shinning, beakers bubbling and racks of multi colored test tubes of unknown substances, line the classroom tables. The students have all been divided up into lab groups. Steven and Tommy are in the back of the room. Sarah's group is at the other end. Steven doesn't get a chance to talk to her before class, but they do exchange glances and grins from across the room.

"Jeez, Steve. In love or what?" Tom smacks Steven on the shoulder.

"Ok, ok. So what. Ya jealous?" Steven asks.

The boys continue to assemble their chemistry experiment.

"I knew it." Tommy whispers under his breath.

They proceed with their experiment. Steven holds up a large test tube as Tom measures two teaspoons of a powdered substance. He then picks up a beaker containing a blue colored liquid and begins to add this to the test tube in Steven's hand. The mixture in the glass test tube starts to react. First just a slight agitation begins, and then it starts to bubble furiously in

Steven's hand. He's not sure if he should continue to hold it or let it drop to the table. When the hot bubbling fluid shoots straight up and out of the test tube, Steven has no choice but to let go. The tube falls and smashes on the floor, sending glass shards in every direction. The blue foaming fluid cascades over their lab table. Steven is stunned. The two chemicals used in the experiment should not have acted to produce this result. Steven looks over at Tom. Tommy is laughing hysterically.

"Smooth move Steven. What did you do?" Tom manages between giggles.

"Nothin. I didn't do a thing." A look of shock is still on Steven's face.

Laughing and loosing his balance, Tommy falls back against the wall. He grabs at Steven's lab coat, trying to steady himself.

"Tommy. What did you put in there?" Steven asks, as he helps Tom to his feet.

"Oh, nothin, just a little food coloring, vinegar and baking soda. I though it would be funny. Jeez. Don't have a heart attack over it."

"Yea, real funny. You clod." Steven counters.

Steven looks up and across the room. Sarah and the rest of the class are all laughing by this time. Sarah had been watching the whole thing from the beginning. She winks at Steven and smiles.

The teacher, Mr. Black, has now become aware of the disturbance in the back of the room.

"Class! Class! If Steven and Mr. Toth are quite done with their little experiment, then, perhaps they would like to take part in ours. Now, if you would all get your chemicals and experiments ready, we should be ready to begin. Unless the two in the back have a problem with that."

"No sir." Steven and Tom answer.

The class resumes. The two boys continue to snicker at each other all the way through class. Finally, the bell rings and the students are dismissed. Sarah has just five minutes between classes. She corners Steven on his way out.

"Steven? Remember I told you that I wanted to talk to you?"

"Oh, sure. Sure, I remember."

"Well, I wanted to ask you something. Will you come over to my house? Tonight, after school, I could really use some help."

"Help with what?" He wanted to know.

"I need help with the games. I have a few more things to put together. My Dad is in town and he's been busy building some of the things I need. I could sure use your help."

Steven had to answer yes this time, having turned Sarah down so many times before. Creepy old house or not, Steven would go this time.

"Sure. I'd like that." Steven tried to sound thrilled.

"I'll call my mom at lunch time and tell her that I will be going over to your house after school."

Sarah was thrilled. She wanted to show Steven a little part of her world. A world quite different then anything Steven will ever see again.

"I'll meet you out by the arch at three fifteen. We can walk to my house. So, I'll see you later." Sarah brushes against Steven as she leaves.

As Steven heads down the hall, to his next class, a hand grabs his shoulder from behind.

"Hey. Hold on." The voice and hand belong to Kevin.

"Was that Sarah Trottier? What are you talking to her for? Jeez. She's kind of weird, don't you think?"

"Leave her alone, Kevin. She's ok." Steven responds.

"What? Why should I? What is she to you?"

Steven can start to feel his anger rising. He tries to respond calmly.

"Nothin we're just friends. You don't have to be so mean to her."

"Yea, maybe I'm wrong about her. But what if I'm not. You know that her whole family is strange. They live up there in that old house on the hill. Nobody has lived there for years. Until, until they moved in last summer. That's why I asked her to be in charge of the spooky entertainment at my party. She's spooky!"

"That's enough. She's not strange. Just leave us alone." Steven was now yelling.

"Holy cow! You like her! Kevin replies.

The two boys walk off in separate directions. Steven is visibly upset at Kevin. He can't believe that his once good friend would treat people like this.

"You're hopeless man!" Kevin shouts back, from down the hall.

Steven does not respond to Kevin. He looks straight ahead. His anger and hurt feelings are right on the surface. He only knows, that Kevin will get his someday.

"You'll be sorry Kevin. You'll be sorry." Steven mumbles as he walks away.

"You'll be sorry…"

"A Watch Pot Never Boils."

* CHAPTER FOUR *

The school bell rings at exactly three fifteen. The quite halls of Whitman High, are suddenly filled with students bursting out of their last class of the day, hurrying to be the first out of the school. Everyone is glad that it is Friday. Finally, the weekend is here, some will be trick-or-treating and others will be attending holiday parties.

Steven had been sitting in his last hour study hall, fumbling with his pencil. He didn't have any homework for the weekend, and sat there thinking what a waste of time this study hall was. His eyes glued to the huge round clock on the wall, Steven watched as the minutes ticked away a bit too slowly, just like the old saying "A watch Pot Never Boils," how true this seemed to Steven. He was anxious to meet Sarah. When the bell did ring, it startled him; the steady ticking of that very same clock had mesmerized him. He was jolted into the present.

Steven was ready to go. His books had been closed and stacked neatly on the top of the desk, just waiting on that darn clock. He was out the door ahead of everyone else, running through the hall and up the stairs, taking them two at a time, Steven reaches his locker on the third floor. Steven's locker is the fifth one from the end, right next to Kevin's. The huge school bell, mounted on the wall over- head, finally ceases its methodical ringing. Steven begins to fumble with the lock. Looking up for a moment, he sees that a folded yellow note is sticking out of the crack of the door. Steven forgets where he was, with his combination lock, he starts over.

"Two full turns to the right and stop at twelve," Steven repeats his combination out loud. "One full turn left and back to twelve and then right to seventeen, there."

Half of the time, the combination locks on these old lockers don't work right, if at all. This time Steven was in luck. The door of his locker clicks and swings open. He grabs the note before it falls to the floor. There are just a few words jotted on the otherwise blank card.

"Don't forget to meet me today after school. I'll be waiting." Steven read the words softly to himself.

Sarah had left him a reminder. He shoves his books into the locker, letting them fall where they may. With one hand, Steven slams the door of his locker and scrambles the dial of his lock.

While neatly folding the note and tucking it into his back pocket, Steven scans up and down the hall, looking for any sight of Kevin. He wants to avoid another confrontation, at all costs. The coast was clear. He hurried down the stairs, ran through the hall, and was out the front door and into the school courtyard in nothing flat.

Steven stood for a moment to catch his breath. He could see that across the school courtyard, Sarah stood waiting under the arch. Steven walked calmly over the stone path; he didn't want to appear too eager.

"There you are, I'm glad you didn't forget, I was afraid that you might." Sarah commented.

"How could I forget. You left me a note," Steven responds.

"I was just making sure." Sarah smiles and holds out her hand. "Shall we?"

Steven, is a little hesitant at first to take her hand, someone might see him.

They start walking, after a few steps, Sarah takes matters into her own hands, so to speak, and grabs Steve's hand and holds it softly but firmly. They continue their walk hand in hand, on their way to the Trottier house.

"The Trotier House."

* CHAPTER FIVE *

Steven had never felt this way about a girl, and yet, here he was, walking side by side, hand in hand with Sarah Trottier. No matter how others had ridiculed and made fun of Sarah, Steven was proud to be walking with her.

"I don't live very far from here." Sarah broke the uncomfortable silence.

"I know. You live in the old Mandrake Mansion. I've seen you walking home from school. What's it like? The old house, what's it like living there?" Steven asked.

"So, you've been following me huh?" joked Sarah.

"No. I live up around on Deedmoore Trail, it's just a few minutes from here," defended Steven.

"Do your parents know that you are coming over to my house?" asked Sarah.

"No. I didn't get a chance to call my mom at lunchtime. But, that's ok. Just as long as I make it home by five o'clock. She always has dinner ready at exactly five."

Steven continued to press Sarah for an answer, "So what's it like living there?"

"It's just an old house, with a lot of cold drafty rooms. Why do you ask?" Sarah wanted to know.

"Do you know the history of that house or the background of the previous owners?" Steven asked as he was silently recalling the stories that he'd always heard as a child.

"No. Tell me." Sarah coaxed Steven on.

"The Mandrakes built the house many years ago. They were the richest people in town. The house sat up on the hill so that Mr. Mandrake could watch over all his property. He owned nearly everything in town. The Mandrakes controlled the banks, bars and stores. When the great depression hit, they lost all of their money. After awhile most people just forgot about the Mandrakes up on the hill. The rumors around town said that Mrs. Mandrake lost her mind and murdered her husband in his sleep. She poured a kettle of boiling candle wax over his face. It filled his mouth, nose and ears. His head was incased in hot wax."

"So what happened to Mrs. Mandrake? Did she go to jail?"

"No," continued Steven. "She just kept her husband in the next bedroom. She died shortly after that. But, it was years before anyone found them. At least that's how the story goes."

"You're making all that up. You're just trying to scare me. You'll see that it takes more than that to frighten me." Sarah assures Steven.

The two children turned the last corner on their way to Sarah's house. Just up ahead, sitting high atop the hill, stood the Mandrake Mansion. Steven had only been in the old house once. That one time was on a dare. Tommy had dared him to go up to a broken window and crawl inside. He was supposed to go in and unlock the front door so that the other kids could come in that way. Once inside the darkened house, something had come over Steven. He panicked and jumped back out through the window.

The house always looked spooky at night. Like many things, cloaked in the darkness of night, our imaginations run wild. This house was different. Even now in the bright afternoon sun, Steven could not help noticing how eerie the place looked.

The house was made of Grey stone. The windows of the mansion were still mostly boarded over. There was one large window that allowed a view of a spiral staircase on the second floor. These stairs seemed to lead to the spire at the top of the house. The spire room is where the Mandrakes had died.

A fence encircled the entire property. As Steven and Sarah were approaching the broken iron gate, Steven saw that there was an old pick up truck and trailer in the driveway. The trailer was painted with outlandish pictures. Pictures of exotic looking creatures and clowns. A banner over the pictures read, "ALIVE AND IN CAPTIVITY. ZAMBORA."

"What's that?" asked Steven.

"My father is home. He'll want to meet you. Come on, I'll race you to the door." With that, Sarah was off, running up the hill, leaving Steven behind.

Sarah stood at the front door of the mansion. "Come on, come on."

Steven made his way to the front door. The door was a huge wooden affair with a lion head protruding from its knocker. Sarah produced a skeleton key from her pocket and inserted it into the rusted door lock. With a creek, the door opened.

"Hurry. Hurry. Come in. Come in." Sarah yanked Steven into the house and slammed the door. "Wait right here. I'll go tell my father that I'm home." Sarah ran off down the hallway and disappeared.

Steven stood in the foyer looking around the old house. The chandelier over his head was covered in cobwebs. No light seemed to penetrate the boarded windows. This cast a gloomy glow of darkness throughout the whole of the house. There were travel trunks, packing crates and boxes lining the hallway. Each box was covered with stickers. A remembrance, perhaps, of the places that they have been.

"Down here, down here." Sarah appeared at the end of the hall. "My father would like to meet you."

Steven walked to where Sarah stood. She took his hand and led him into the other room. "Right in here. My father is in his study."

Steven could not have been prepared for what he was about to see. Sitting behind a desk at the far end of the room was a giant of a man. It was not the size of the man that startled Steven. Rather, it was his appearance. He was dressed in a fine suit with white gloves. Nothing strange about that. It was his face. His face was covered with a clown mask that looked out of place with his attire.

"Father, this is the boy I told you about. Steven say hello to my father." Sarah handled the introductions.

"Hello Mr. Trottier." Steven managed.

The man slowly looked up from the papers on the desk. His clown face and eyes were fixated on Steven. After a long silence he spoke.

"You like my daughter?" Sarah's father asked in a thick voice. "You like to stay with us?"

Steven wasn't sure how to answer. What did he mean, by asking if he wanted to stay with them?

"No father. Steven is here to help me with the party games. You remember." Sarah broke in. "We will be in my room working."

"Good to meet you Steven." Mr. Trottier extended his white, gloved hand to Steven. "Welcome young man." With that he sat back down and resumed looking over the papers on his desk.

Sarah led Steven back to the hall and over to the spiral staircase. The staircase dominated the center of the house.

"His clown face and eyes were fixated on Steven."

Steven wasn't sure if he wanted to go up those stairs. He had already seen things that made him question his decision to come here in the first place. But still, he did like Sarah and that was the most important thing. What would he find at the top of the stairs? This was after all, the place where Mrs. Mandrake and her husband had been found rotting away together. Steven braced himself and followed Sarah up the winding staircase. There were pictures hanging on the wall to the side of the stairs. Steven could only catch fleeting images in the dim light of the house. Images of what looked to be clowns in make up and costume. There was writing under each painting. Perhaps the name of each character was printed there.

The top of the stairs emptied out into another hall. Each side of the hall had one door. The door on the left was open. There was a crackling noise coming from inside the room. A hissing and crackling that put Steven on edge. Sarah took Steven's hand and led the way to her bedroom door. The closed door on the right side of the hall. As Sarah was fumbling with the lock on her door, Steven tried to catch a peek into the room across the way. He backed up just enough as to give him a clear view of the interior of the room. The hissing was coming from a television. There was no picture, just static and snow as if the channel had signed off the air. Sitting in front of the screen was a hooded figure, shrouded in black. Whoever this was, they just sat there starring into the blank television.

"That's my mother." Sarah said as she reached in front of Steven and closed the door. "She has a very rare skin problem. She has to stay out of the light."

"Oh. I see." Steven really didn't see how that explained the television and no picture.

"Over here. Let's go into my room." Sarah opened the door and invited Steven inside.

Once inside, Steven's eyes lit up. Sarah's room stood in stark contrast to the rest of the neglected mansion. The room was bright with cheery sunshine and flowers. Brightly striped wallpaper and a floor that looked freshly waxed, expanded in front of Steven. There were mirrors of every type and size lining the room. A full-length mirror stood upright in the corner of the room. This one seemed to be much, much older then the rest. An antique perhaps. Sarah would occasionally look at the mirror. Steven wasn't sure if she was looking at her own reflection or searching for something else in its depths.

"I see you like my mirror," Sarah says after seeing Steven's interest in the old object.

"It is very unique," he remarks.

"This mirror is one of a large group, that was handed down to my father. It is said, that his great ancestors had constructed them out of the very finest glass and silver. These mirrors are believed to be some of the very first ever made. For many years, they had been stored away, until my father presented them to me. Would you like to see something?" she asks.

Before Steven has a chance to answer, Sarah waves her hand across the surface of the mirror. It begins to shimmer with a light of its own.

"Wow, what is that?" Steven is fascinated by what he sees.

"Oh, I'll show you even more if you want, but not right now," she waves her hand across the mirror once more and the eerie light subsides.

Shelves separated the mirrors. Little dolls occupied these places of honor. Steven notices one detail of the dolls. They all seem to have the likeness of Alice in wonderland. Then Steven realizes that Sarah, with her blond hair tied up and her apron smock dress also has that same likeness. The room was right out of "ALICE THROUGH THE LOOKING GLASS", mirrors and all. There is a chair in the corner that is in the shape of a toadstool. The stool is next to a small table that has been set for a tea party.

"Care for some tea?" asks Sarah.

Steven stands stunned by all of this.

Sarah walks behind Steven and closes her bedroom door.

"So. I guess you have a lot of questions by now." Sarah's statement was the understatement of the century. Steven had a lot of questions that needed some answers. He scarily thought that anything could explain away the sights he had just witnessed.

"What is with your dad? Why didn't he take off that clown mask when he met me? What was your mom watching on that blank television screen? And why are there so many crates and boxes down stairs in the hall?" Steven had rattled off all of these questions, without even stopping for a breath of air.

"Woe, slow down there. Let me explain as best as I can," Sarah removed some stuffed rabbits from her bed, "Come. Sit

34

here beside me," she patted the space next to her. Steven walked over and sat beside her.

"Do you remember me telling you that my father was in the entertainment business?" Sarah asked. "Well, let me see if I can explain. Many years ago, when my father was a young man, he traveled with the biggest circus in Europe. His family was known all over as the FLYING TROTTIERS, they were the best high wire and trapeze artists in the world. My father was the youngest of five boys. There was one stunt that the family featured, as they're most thrilling and dangerous. My father and two of his brothers would all balance bicycles on the high wire. They would then place a board along their shoulders. This allowed his other two brothers to balance their bikes on the plank of wood. My grandmother would then stand on one of the boy's shoulders and my grandfather would stand on the other. After all were balanced, they would pedal the bikes across the wire and back. On one fateful night, while performing their signature stunt, my father lost control of his bike. He fought to regain his balance. It was too late. The wire shook violently, his brothers and parents fell seventy-five feet to the ground. In that one instant, his whole family and everything he knew, came to an end. My father stayed on with the circus as a clown. He could not bare the shame he felt. So, to hide his true feelings and face, he had that clown makeup tattooed to his skin forever. That wasn't a mask, Steven. That was my fathers face of shame."

"Oh, I'm sorry. I didn't mean to be rude. It just looked so strange." Steven added.

"Anyway, a few years later while traveling in the Congo, my father met his bride to be. My mother's name is Zambora."

"Yes, I saw that name painted on the side of that trailer out front." Steven offered.

Sarah continued her story. She went on to explain that her mother had been born with a rare disease of the skin. At certain times of the year, her body would grow an enormous amount of hair. She would literally be transformed into an APE WOMAN.

"I guess that I still don't quite understand," said Steven as he looked into Sarah's soft eyes.

"My Father now runs a sideshow business. We travel all over with our show." Sarah pauses for a moment and takes Steven's hand. "I wish we could have met sooner. We are getting ready to move again. That's why the hall down stairs is jammed with crates. Maybe, like my father asked you, YOU STAY WITH US?"

Steven began to laugh, until he realized that Sarah was not kidding. There was allot that Steven didn't understand, and whether he knew it or not, Sarah intended on taking Steven with her and her family, even if it meant against his will.

"Yea, maybe," he answered.

The time was getting late and Steven would have to be going soon.

"I'm sorry that I didn't get to help you with your party games, we got too busy talking." Steven stood and walked to the bedroom door.

"Oh, you helped." Sarah led Steven down the spiral stairs and out the front door. She kissed Steven on the cheek "You think about what my father and I asked you."

"You mean, come with you? I don't know." Steven stepped off of the porch. "I'll see you tomorrow at Kevin's then?" Steven changed the subject.

"Yes, yes, I'll see you then." Sarah turned and went into the house.

As Steven left the fenced yard, he heard Sarah slam the heavy door of the mansion.

Once inside, Sarah stood at the small window along side of the door. She watched as Steven walked through the rickety old gate and out onto the sidewalk in front of the mansion.

Suddenly, the sound of screeching tires pierced the air. A speeding car came racing down the street. The car made a purposeful swerve to the wrong side of the road. Steven had to step back from the curb as the car came roaring towards him. A barrage of eggs is launched from the car. Yokes and runny clear matter, blanket the sidewalk at Steven's feet. His quick stepping reflexes have saved him from being pelted with the white missiles. Steven recognizes the car and two of the four boys in it. Carl Biggons, one of the seniors on the football team, was driving. Steven felt a deep hurt as he realized one of the boys in the backseat was Kevin. Not only that, Kevin was one of the ones throwing the eggs. Steven wondered why Kevin would do such a thing.

Sarah watched in silent rage from her vantagepoint at the window. She watched as the car sped away. She watched and could feel the hurt and humiliation. Sarah was all too familiar with these very same feelings.

"I'll take care of them. They'll see." Sarah was talking out loud. "My sweet Steven. My sweet Steven. Don't you worry."

Steven bent down and brushed a few stray eggshells from the cuff of his pants. He glanced over his shoulder in both directions. The coast was clear.

Steven continued his short walk home, trying to sort things out in his head. Things like; did Kevin know that the boy on the sidewalk was his onetime friend? Why had Kevin done this to him? Or, maybe the boys in the car were just out blowing off steam after football practice. Maybe they hadn't recognized him. Then again, maybe they did.

"He was more then three hours late for dinner."

* CHAPTER SIX *

"Eight twenty." Steven noted the time as he entered his house. He was late for dinner. He was more then three hours late for dinner. His father would be upset about this. One thing that his father insisted on was that dinner be served at precisely five o'clock sharp and that Steven be there on time.

Steven's day had already been pretty tough. He didn't need the scorn that he would surely receive from his father. The only bright spot of his day had been the time that he spent with Sarah Trottier.

The smell of Mexican food filled the house. Steven loved his mom's home made tacos.

"Is that you Steven? Go wash your hands and come down to dinner, I'll warm some up for you," Steven's mother yelled from the kitchen. "It's a good thing your father isn't here. You being late and all."

Steven rushed to his room and flopped down on his bed. He had gotten a reprieve. He wouldn't have to sit through dinner listening to his father go on and on about his being late.

Steven got up and went to the bathroom at the end of the hall, and washed up for dinner.

"So where's dad tonight?" Steven asked as he entered the dinning room.

"He got called out of town at the last minute. Your father had to fly to Houston to meet a special client. Here Hun, sit down." She pulled the chair out for Steven.

A large plate of homemade tacos and tostados sat in the middle of the table. Steven took a few of each and placed them on his plate. His mother came around from the other side of the table to sit closer to Steven.

"Steven, I have something very important to tell you. I want you to listen carefully. Your father just got his promotion as head of development for overseas business at his company. This means that we are going to have to move to Japan. Well, just your father and I will be going. Your father thought that it might be best to enroll you into a military school out on the East Coast. He felt that the discipline would do you good."

All Steven seemed to hear were the two most dreaded words in the English language. His father had always been against public schools and wanted to put Steven into a military academy. He used those words to threaten Steven whenever he screwed up. Not that there is anything wrong with military schools. Steven was just not the type.

"Put the boy into the Academy. That'll make a man out of him." Steven could here his father saying those very words. It was always his mother that would stick up for him. It would seem that she could no longer keep Steven out of Military School.

"There isn't much time either." Steven's mother continued. "Your father and I have to be in London next week. From there we fly on to Japan. All of the plans and arrangements have already been made for your transfer to Culver Military Academy. You'll be starting at Culver after the holiday break in December. Until then, you can stay with your aunt and finish this semester."

Steven was in shock. He could only sit in disbelief at what he had just heard. Suddenly, the Mexican feast in front of him no longer looked that appetizing. After a few moments of silence, Steven finally spoke up.

"But Mom! I can't go to one of those military schools. I won't fit in. Why can't I go with you and dad?"

"I'm sorry dear, that's just not possible. Your father and I will be transferring from one place to another. We can't be bothered with enrolling you into a new school every time we move. It is the best way for all of us."

"You mean the best way for you and dad. You said it yourself. You can't be bothered with me."

Steven pushed his plate aside and stood up from the table. As far as he was concerned, this conversation was over. He turned to leave the room.

"Get back here right now." Steven's mother demanded.

"I'm not going to that place. There's no way. You can make all of the plans and arrangements that you want. But your mistaken if you think that you can just ship me off."

"Steven. You will not talk to me like that and just walk away. You will do as you are told. Now come back over here and sit down."

Steven ignored his mother and continued walking out of the room. His mother was furious. He had never seen her so mad. As Steven started up the stairway to his room, he remembered Sarah and Mr. Trottier's offer. Maybe he would go with them.

Steven entered his bedroom and slammed the door behind him. The wall shook from the force. The louder the door slammed the better. Steven wanted his mother to hear it. He planted himself on the edge of his bed. The only thing on his mind was running away. Far, far away. If there had been somewhere to run to right then, Steven would have already been on his way. No matter what he had to do, he was not going to be sent away as a convenience to his parents.

Steven grabbed one of the comic books from the pile that covered his bed. He could always escape to the safety of his books. It wasn't long before Steven fell asleep. Safe for now, in a land of dreams.

"A ribbon for Sarah's hair."

* CHAPTER SEVEN *

October 1957
Saturday Morning.

A loud sound startled Steven from his sleep. There was a roar in the hall outside of his bedroom door. It took a few minutes for Steven to shake the dullness of sleep from his head. Now he recognized the sound in the hall. It was the growl of his mom running the Hoover vacuum.

Steven rolled over on his side to look at the Mickey Mouse clock on his dresser. According to Mickey, it was six o'clock. One hand up and one hand down. Steven covered his head with the sheet and tried to block the obtrusive noise of the sweeper in the hall.

"No one should have to get up at six in the morning on a Saturday." Steven mumbled to himself.

No sooner had he closed his eyes under the shield of his sheet, than a voice from the other side of the door called out.

"Steven? Are you getting up?" Steven's mother knocked on the door. "Come on. There's lots of work to do today. Come on. It's time you got up."

Steven could hear his mom walk off and go down stairs. He raised himself up and sat on the edge of his bed. Had it all been a bad dream or something. Perhaps that was it. Surely he wasn't going to be sent off to live with an aunt that he didn't even know and have to go to a military school. This had to be a terrible nightmare.

Steven sat there with his head in his hands. The cobwebs of sleep were slowly clearing. He tried to recollect what had taken place last night. No. It hadn't been a dream. The reality of it was a slap to Steven's senses.

"You getting up?" his mother yelled from the bottom of the stairs.

"Yea. Give me a minute." Steven yelled back.

After washing and brushing his teeth, Steven got dressed. His mother was waiting at the bottom of the stairs. She clutched a piece of notepaper in one hand and a broom in the other. As he was coming down the stairs she handed the paper to him.

"This is a list of chores you have to get done today. The house has to be spotless before the real estate agent gets here this afternoon. She may have a buyer for the house. You need to get the leaves raked and mow the grass. When you get that done, go out to the garage and sweep it out. Throw away any trash and straighten up in there."

"But mom, remember, I'm going to Kevin's party tonight. Before the party I wanted to go over to the five and dime to buy a gift for Sarah. The store closes today at noon."

"If you don't get all of your work done, your not going anywhere. So you better get started."

Steven looked at the list and then back at his mother. He decided to keep his mouth shut. There would be no pleading his side. His parents had made up their mind. They were moving and planned to send him away.

"Go have yourself some breakfast and then get busy on that list." Steven's mother resumed her cleaning.

Steven did as his mother said. After a quick glass of orange juice he headed out to the garage to get the rake and mower. At least someone was on his side, because the wind had already blown most of the leaves into the neighbor's yard. Steven figured he could skip the raking and just mow the yard.

The garage was next on the list. Steven looked at the huge mound of clutter that filled the inside. Old toys, broken tools, boxes of old newspapers, the place was a mess. He started by hauling all the boxes of newspapers out to the alley behind the house. The papers had been stored for an upcoming school paper drive. A school that Steven would no longer be attending after this semester.

Steven moved everything left in the garage over to one side and started to sweep the floor. He worried that this was going to take to much time and that he would not get to the store before they closed. He stopped sweeping and leaned against the broom handle. Steven looked out of the door to see if there was any sight of his mother. The coast seemed to be clear. He threw the broom to the floor and crossed to the other side of the garage to get his bicycle. He would ride down to the store and be back before his mother missed him. Steven waited to get on the bike. He pushed his bike to the alley, being careful not to be seen. Swinging his leg over the seat, Steven was off to buy the perfect gift for Sarah.

Williams Five and Ten Cent Store was only about a mile away. It was at the bottom of Miami Street along with a few other small shops. Steven coasted down the steep street and was at the store in no time at all. He secured his bike to the bike rack and ran inside. Steven knew just what kind of gift he wanted to get. The perfect gift for Sarah would be a beautiful new hair ribbon. Not just any ribbon would do. This ribbon had to be made of the finest red satin. Steven looked around for Mr. Williams, the owner and clerk of the little store. Mr. Williams was busy behind the cash register at the other side of the store.

"Afternoon Mr. Williams. Not closing yet are you?" Steven said as he approached the counter.

"Hello Steven. No, I'm not closing quite yet. I was just going over the morning's receipts. Was there something I could help you find?"

Steven put both hands on the counter top and leaned toward Mr. Williams.

"Yes, yes if you could. I want to buy a gift for someone special. A want a fine satin ribbon. You know the kind that girls wear in their hair. And it has to be red. Do you have that?" Steven asked eagerly.

"Right over here." Mr. Williams stepped out from behind the counter. "Here we are." He directed Steven's attention to the brightly colored ribbons hanging from a hook. Removing the whole bunch from the hook, Mr. Williams presented Steven with the rainbow of streamers.

"I'll take that one." Steven pointed at the deep red one. "That's the one."

Mr. Williams pulled the selected ribbon from the bunch.

"Will there be anything else?" he asked.

"No. That's it. How much is it?"

"Thirty five cents should cover it." Mr. Williams placed the ribbon into a small brown paper bag as Steven slapped a quarter and a dime onto the counter.

"Here you go," he said as he extended the bagged gift to Steven.

"Thank you Mr. Williams." Steven clutched the bag and started for the door.

As he was opening the door to leave, he spotted Kevin coming up the walk outside.

Steven wanted to avoid any kind of confrontation. He thought maybe, Kevin hadn't seen him. He would have no such luck.

"Steven. Hey Steven. Wait up." Kevin yelled to get Steven's attention.

"I want to talk to you."

Steven got to his bike and proceeded to ride away. He decided to act as if he hadn't heard Kevin.

"Steven, please, I wanted to apologize to you." Kevin continued to yell with his hands in the air.

Steven was out of range and did not hear. He was concentrating on getting back home before he was missed.

Kevin hadn't realized until after the eggs were thrown, that the boy in front of the old Trottier house was Steven. He was just having some fun with a few of the older football players. He never meant to hurt Steven or anyone else for that matter. Kevin wanted to make up with Steven. He was ashamed of the way he had been treating Steven. Kevin lowered his arms and stood watching as Steven rode away. Kevin figured that he would apologize to Steven tonight at his party. That is, if Steven still wanted to come to the party. Kevin wouldn't blame him if he didn't.

Steven peddled his bike up the alley and into the garage. The trip to the store surely hadn't taken more than twenty minutes. Leaning his bicycle against the wall, Steven was startled by his mother's voice.

"Oh, there you are. I was looking for you."

Steven was sure that he had been caught. Before turning to face his mother, Steven stuffed the paper shopping bag under his jacket.

"I was just…" Steven stammered.

"Well, I see that you have most of your work done." She interrupted Steven. "Go ahead and finish up in here and that should do it."

"Ah, ah, ok." Steven had pulled it off. His mother had not seen him leave on his bike.

"And by the way, the realtor isn't coming until tomorrow," she added before walking back to the house.

"That figures." Steven remarked in a voice to low to be heard. There was a faint smile on his face. He resumed sweeping the garage floor.

"Kevin's house looked like spook central."

* CHAPTER EIGHT *

October 1957.
Saturday, early evening.

Steven stands in front of his closet trying to decide what he should wear to Kevin's party. If it had been a costume party like years past, the question of what to wear would not be a problem. Steven had already prepared to go dressed as Zorro, sword and all. But now, he had to try and look cool for the party. He wanted to look good especially for Sarah. Steven selected a new pair of starched, straight leg jeans from the closet and laid them across the bed. A plain white tee shirt is placed on top of the jeans. Steven's new pair of black, high top, red ball jets completes the ensemble.

Steven looks at his Mickey Mouse clock and sees that it is now ten tell six and there is just enough time for him to get cleaned up before Tommy arrives at seven. After bathing, Steven takes special care in combing his hair and even though he doesn't shave yet, he splashes a handful of his father's aftershave onto his face. Steven hurries to get dressed, but he takes the time to make sure that his pant cuffs are turned up nice and even a full four inches. He stands in front of the mirror admiring his new look. Steven pretends to roll a pack of imaginary cigarettes into his shirtsleeve. He steps back for one more look in the mirror.

"Not bad. Not bad at all," he remarks to himself. He is pleased that he no longer looks like a geek.

At precisely seven o'clock, the doorbell rings at the Boskowitz house. Steven hears his mother answer the door.

"Tommy come on in. I'll get Steven for you. He should be about ready. Just have a seat here in the hall chair, I'll be right back," with that, she turns and runs up the stairs to Steven's room.

Steven is just finishing. He grabs a small, black, backpack that he uses for camping and stuffs a few items of clothing into it. Sarah's hair ribbon goes neatly on top. The bag is closed up and Steven is ready to go.

"Steven, Tommy is down stairs. If you still want to go, you better get moving," his mother announces as she bursts into Steven's room.

Steven hides the small backpack from his mother as he walks out of his bedroom.

"And remember young man, you better be back here before midnight or you'll never go out again," she adds as she points a finger in Steven's direction.

"Yea, I know, I know." Steven's reply is a little indignant.

Steven takes the stairs two at a time and motions to Tommy, who is still sitting at the bottom of the stairs.

"Let's go." Steven takes Tommy by the arm of his leather jacket and escorts him rapidly out the front door.

"What's the rush?" Tommy asks. "You got us out of there, like the house was on fire."

"Sorry about that. Things are getting a little strange around here."

"So what's in the bag?" Tommy continues with his questioning.

As the two boys start walking, Steven tells Tommy of his parent's plan to send him away to Culver Military School next semester.

"So what are you going to do Steve?"

"I'm not sure. But one thing I am sure of, is that I am not going to military school. And I'm not going to go back home so that they can send me away." Steven holds his backpack up with one hand, "You see, I brought all I need. I'm not going home."

"Wow. Your serious." Tommy doesn't know what to say.

It's Halloween night. The wind whips at the piles of leaves raked along the curb. A steady flow of costumed children crisscrosses the street, scurrying from house to house begging for treats. Each house displays a Jack-o-lantern to greet the tricksters, little ferries, pirates and bums.

Steven and Tommy continue their walk to Kevin's house. Tommy takes a comb from his back pocket and drags it through his hair. He uses his other hand to smooth a stubborn cowlick into place with a little spit.

"Hey. Got to look good for the chicks." Tommy can't resist teasing Steven. "So, big man, what are you and Sarah going to do tonight?" Tom nudges an elbow at Steve's side as they make their way up the cobblestone walkway to Kevin's front door.

"Wow. Looks like spook central," says Steven.

The house and yard are decorated with pumpkins, ghosts and goblins. There is even a make believe cemetery in one part of the yard. The outside of the house is lit up with eerie red and blue lights, while pounding music reverberates from within. Steven and Tommy enter along with several others. The inside of the house is darkened and decorated with the same Halloween spirit. There are crowds of kids moving in and out of every room. Kevin appears in the doorway wearing his football letter jacket.

"Glad to see that you guys finally made it. Everyone's here." Kevin puts his arm around Steven's shoulder and pulls him close.

"Listen Steven, I'm really sorry about the other day. I wanted to tell you that this morning. I've really been a jerk lately. I just wanted you to know."

Steven pats Kevin on the back as a way of accepting his apology.

"Sarah's out in the kitchen my man. Ya gonna go say hi?" Kevin continues as he pushes Steven in the direction of the kitchen.

"Don't push, I'll go. Leave me alone will you. Jeez."

Sarah is busy in the kitchen. She stands at the refrigerator removing something from one of the shelves. Her back is to Steven as he walks up behind her.

"Trick or Treat."

Sarah is startled and drops the ice cube tray from her hands. Cubes slide across the floor in every direction.

"You scarred me. Now help me clean this mess up." Sarah smiles at Steven.

Steven grabs a nearby bowl to put the stray ice cubes in. The two are kneeling side by side on the floor. Sarah sees that

Steven is feeling a bit uncomfortable and shy. She gently puts her hand on Steven's arm.

"You don't have to be afraid of me. I'm not going to bite you. Even if it is Halloween."

Steven laughs and begins to loosen up. He hands the bowl of ice to Sarah.

"So, what are you doing in here? Making drinks for everyone?" Steven asks.

"Oh, no, the ice is for one of the games. I made up a limited number of admission tickets for each of the games and handed them out to everyone. That way, a different group of kids take part in each of the games. No one has the same experience. Come on, I'll show you." Steven slings his black bag over one shoulder. Sarah takes his hand and leads the way through the house, to a bedroom in the back.

There is a girl standing in the hall taking tickets. Sarah closes the door behind Steven. The room is very dark and quiet. The only light in the room comes from a single candle; its flickering flame dances shadows on the walls. Steven squints in the darkness. It takes a few moments to adjust. He begins to make out the image of a simple wooden chair in the center of the room.

There are others in the room. They step away from their places against the wall. One youth is blindfolded and placed in the wooden chair.

"Watch this." Sarah whispers to Steven.

"Isn't that John Sites?" Steven recognizes John from school.

"Shhh—, watch." Sarah puts a finger to her lips.

Steven watches as six other kids form a circle around the chair. Steven has never seen any of these kids before. This seems odd to him. He watches and listens as the circle of strangers begin to chant.

"We're going to burn you. We're going to burn you. We're going to burn you good. We're going to burn you with this hot burning coal!"

The chanting went on for several minutes. The same, droning melody, over and over.

"We're going to burn you. We're going to burn you. We're going to burn you good. We're going to burn you with this hot burning coal."

A small, slender boy comes from out of the darkness. He takes an ice cube from the bowl that Sarah holds in her outstretched hand. He returns to the circle of other chanters and continues one more time.

"We're going to burn you. We're going to burn you. We're going to burn you good. We're going to burn you with this hot burning coal."

This time, as the last line is chanted, the ice cube is held against the blindfolded victim's bare arm.

"And it's going to BURN!"

John leaps from the chair, stripping the blindfold from his eyes.

"What the—you burnt me! Stop it. Are you crazy?" He shouts wildly, as his arm welts up, as if burnt by a red-hot coal.

The boy with the ice shows John what was truly placed against his arm.

"Good God, you guys. That really felt hot." John says as he begins to calm down.

"He's a good subject. Don't you think? He scares easy." Sarah whispers to Steven.

"Yea, I wouldn't fall for that stuff." Steven boasts.

Sarah takes Steven's hand once again, "We've got some more games in the other room, come on I'll show you."

They stop in the hall for a brief moment to allow another group of kids to squeeze by. Steven looks down the hall and listens; there is a strange chanting coming from the room at the other end of the hall. Steven looks back at Sarah; she has been studying Steven intently. Her eyes glued to his features.

"I'm glad I found you Steven." She winks at him and they continue down the hall to the second bedroom.

This room is just as dark as the first. Once again, time is needed for the eyes to adjust. Steven and Sarah join with the group of kids in the center of the room.

"Do you want to try this one?" Sarah asks of Steven.

"No, no, that's ok. I'll just watch this time. You go ahead, if you want to. I'll stand back here against the wall and stay out of the way."

A girl named Karla was selected from the group. She is instructed to lie down across two folding chairs, her head at one end and her feet at the other. There is nothing supporting her middle. She is suspended between the two chairs.

A small circle is formed around the two chairs. Steven watches as Sarah chants with the group.

"Stiff as a board, stiff as a board, your body is stiff as a board. Straight as a nail, straight as a nail, your body is straight as a nail. Light as a feather, light as a feather, your body is like a feather."

After several minutes of this, two boys on either end of Karla, reach down and place a single finger under each of her armpits and one under the back of each knee. They proceed to lift Karla straight into the air. She remains stiff as a board. The boys slowly lower her back to the chairs. Karla jumps up to a round of laughter and applause.

"Mind over matter," she exclaims.

The others exit the room, leaving Steven and Sarah alone in the dark. Sarah joins Steven in the back of the room.

"Well, you seem to be having a good time." Steven smiles and takes Sarah by both hands. Sarah moves in close and looks into his eyes.

"You know, your becoming very special to me." She leans in slowly and the two kiss.

"I'm sorry. But, I had to do that." Sarah apologizes.

"Don't be. I liked it. I was wondering if I could kiss you."

"You may." Sarah smiles.

They embrace and Steven kisses her in earnest. They look at each other for what seems eternity. Finally, Sarah pulls Steven out the door and into the hallway.

"Come on, there's one more room that you have got to see."

Kevin and Tommy are coming down the hall from the other direction. The four meet. Kevin is the first to speak.

"Say! You two seem to be hitting it off." He winks at Steven.

"Yea. We haven't seen you guys all night," adds Tommy.

"Nock it off you guys." Steven pulls Sarah close to him. "She's just been showing me her games."

"Yea, I'll bet she has. I'm just kidding." Kevin is quick to add.

Tommy points at a room down the hall. "Hey, what's in that room?" He starts to head in the direction of the closed door at the end of the hall. Sarah stops him cold. She grabs him by the back of his arm.

"Wait! You'll have to wait your turn to see that one. I was going to show Steven first."

"Yea, what have you got down there?" Kevin asks.

"Tell you what…you wait right here and when I'm done with Steven…" Sarah pauses and then chooses just the right words. "…I'll come back and COLLECT you."

Steven and Sarah continue walking toward the door at the end of the hall.

"What did you mean by telling Kevin and Tommy that you would be back to COLLECT them? You said it in such a strange serious way."

"You'll see soon enough. Don't worry, I'm not going to hurt YOU." Sarah replies.

Steven trusts Sarah, but there was something sinister in the tone of her voice that made him feel uneasy. He didn't know what to expect next or what Sarah was really capable of. "What was she up to?" Steven asked himself.

"Go ahead and open it.   Don't be afraid."

* CHAPTER NINE *

Steven and Sarah stood motionless in front of the door at the end of the hall. Steven slowly extended his right hand and took a solid grip on the doorknob. He hesitated slightly before turning the knob.

"Go ahead and open it. Don't be afraid. I told you that I wouldn't hurt you. Now go on in." Sarah pushes.

The door swings open with ease. Steven steps into the darkened room ever so cautiously. This room is different some how. It is quite dark and empty, except for some drape cloaked object in the center of the room, gone are all of the other kids.

"Oh, I know. You wanted to make out in this room." Steven jokes.

"No silly. Come over here and I'll try to explain." The two sit on a small couch in the corner of the dark room. Sarah asks Steven if he had given any thought to the question that her father had asked him the other night. Did he want to go with them or not. A lot of things had changed in Steven's life since the other night. Had he not packed a bag for just that reason?

"I will come with you and your family. There is nothing for me in this place," Steven says.

"Good, I'm so glad you said that. Remember the tickets that I printed up for these games? Well, there are only two tickets to this room. I had one for you," she waves a ticket in the air at Steven, "and the other I gave to Kevin. You won't be in need of a ticket. You volunteered to go with me."

Sarah explained a few more things to Steven in the privacy of the darkened room. After a few moments the two kissed. With Steven's help, they uncovered the hulking object in the center of the room. The object turned out to be the old antique mirror that Steven had observed back in Sarah's bedroom. He remembered now, that Sarah had set up some kind of altar in front of that mirror. He had noticed candles and incense offerings, around the mirror, but at the time, had thought very little about them. Now he understood. Steven unscrewed a couple of bolts from each side of the object and it was freed from its retrains. They laid the object flat on the floor and covered it once again with the black cloth. Sarah gave Steven a few more brief instructions and told him to go stand at the back of the room and watch. She was going to show Steven how she intended to "COLLECT" Kevin.

Sarah opens the door to find that Tommy has disappeared. He had run off to the kitchen to find something to munch on. Kevin stood waiting by himself in the hall.

"Do you have your ticket?" she asks of Kevin. He reaches into his back pocket and produces the hand made ticket.

"You mean this one?" He displays the ticket to Sarah.

"Yes, yes, here, come this way," she says, as she takes the ticket from Kevin.

Sarah backs into the room and summons Kevin to follow. She leads him to the center of the room. As his eyes grow accustomed to the lack of light, he sees the mirror on the floor. "Where is everyone? Where is Steven?" he asks.

"Oh, Steven is here. Say something Steven."

Steven's voice emanates from the darkness, "Hello, Kevin."

Sarah guides Kevin to the edge of the mirror. "What is it supposed to do?" he asks.

"You have to do ten push-ups on the mirror, while repeating a mystical chant," Sarah responds. She pushes Kevin just a little bit closer to the silvery edge. "Come on, try it. No one else will see."

Kevin gives in to Sarah's coaxing. "Ok, I'll try it. What am I supposed to say?"

Happy that Kevin is willing to play along with her little game, Sarah hands Kevin a slip of paper. The paper contains the chant. He studies the words on the paper.

"So, what happens after I say this?" Kevin asks.

"Just try it, you'll see. Don't be afraid. Where's that big brave football player?" Sarah pokes at Kevin with her finger.

"I'm not afraid, it's just that I feel like such a fool doing this. But, I'll play along."

Kevin proceeds to get in a push-up position, on top of the prone mirror. He realizes what a strange sensation it is, to see himself, starring back at himself. Sarah moves back into the darkness along with Steven. She tightens her lips in anticipation, as Kevin begins his first of ten push-ups.

"MIRROR MIRROR, MEN IN THE MIRROR,
MIRROR MIRROR, COME THEE NEAR."

Kevin's eyes are fixed on his reflection, as it seems to draw near and then drifts far. He continues his chanting and pushing.

"MIRROR MIRROR, MEN IN THE MIRROR,
MIRROR MIRROR, COME THEE NEAR."

This is no longer a joke to Kevin. He has lost the smile that permeated his face earlier this night. The look of determination has taken over. As Kevin completes his fifth push-up, a slight sweat now beads on his brow. He continues in a softer more determined tone.

"MIRROR MIRROR, MEN IN THE MIRR..." he stops suddenly in mid chant by the sight of a brief swirl of color in the depths of the mirror. The color disappeared as quickly as it had come. Kevin is not sure if he really saw what he saw. He pauses for a moment. He is noticeably out of breath.

"Please continue Kevin," Sarah's voice breaks the brief silence.

Kevin does as he is told.

"MIRROR MIRROR, MEN IN THE MIRROR,
MIRROR MIRROR, COME THEE NEAR."

As Kevin reaches his tenth and final push-up, the swirl of light and color returns to the mirror. The light grows in its intensity and begins to pulse wildly. The light dances on the walls and ceiling. A green mist fills the room with an unworldly glow. Kevin is caught up in the game. He is oblivious to all that is around him. Sarah clutches Steven's hand, "Now watch, my love. Watch as I COLLECT KEVIN."

Steven can only stand by and watch in disbelief. In the blink of an eye, a shapeless arm reaches up for Kevin. It extends out from the depths of the mirror. Wrapping its long bony fingers around Kevin's wrists, he is dragged screaming and kicking into the mirror itself. Kevin's image and soul become one with the surface of the mirror. The whole process took only but a few seconds. The haze in the room cleared and all is silent.

Sarah brings Steven over to stand with her beside the mirror. They both peer into the mirror. Kevin is in the mirror, clawing in silence, at the inside surface. Sarah bends over and touches the reflection of Kevin.

"There, there, it's alright. I'll add you to my very special COLLECTION. You can be with us always." Sarah looks up at Steven, she smiles wildly, "with us always."

The image of Kevin drifts further back into the silver depths of the mirror, lost in its void of nothingness.

Steven and Sarah lift the mirror from the floor and stand it upright again. They take special care to re-secure it to its ornate frame. Steven tightens the side bolts as Sarah retrieves the black cloth. The mirror is covered once again.

"Their truck pulled out to join up with the caravan."

EPILOGUE
(**epilogue n.** a short concluding section of a book etc.)

Present day.

It is a hot August day, in the late afternoon at the carnival grounds. Dust blows through the fields, that just last night, had been packed with throngs of happy people. Gone are the giggling kids waiting to be next on rides. There is no smell of cotton candy or any of the other carnival delights. It is moving day for the carnival. The colorful tents are all being taken down and rolled up. The carnival food vending trailers have all been packed up tight. Workmen busy themselves by dismantling all of the rides and sideshow attractions, loading the iron beams, the cars for each ride and the neon colored lights onto more then a dozen trucks. As each truck is loaded, it heads out the main gate of the fairgrounds, to join the long caravan on their way to another state, another city, and another County Fair.

One lone truck is the last to finish loading. It's big, sleek and black. There are painted banners on either side of the trailer. The banner on the right side is ablaze with color. A background of yellow, green and red jungle foliage with the words, "ZAMBORA! ALIVE AND CAGED," scrawled across it. The other side of the truck has but a simple black and white sign, with just three words, "HOUSE OF MIRRORS." There is a woman, and a gruff looking man standing at the rear of the truck.

Sarah is much older now. Her once blonde hair, that has turned a dirty shade of Grey, is still tied up by a ribbon. A tattered, red satin ribbon. She is busy with the last few mirrors to be loaded.

"Hand me those two packing pads," she demands of the man assisting her.

He picks up the packing pads with his sweaty grease stained fingers, and walks them over to Sarah.

"Are you about ready to go dear?" he asks.

"Right after we clean this last mirror and get it packed away. You can go ahead and warm up the truck, and then come back here to help me," Sarah suggests.

"Good. I'm ready to get out of this town," he says as he wipes chewing tobacco spit from his chin. "Suits me just fine." He opens the door to the truck cab and raises himself up. There are several stacks of comic books on the seat. He pushes them to the side and settles behind the big steering wheel. With one turn of the key, the engine roars to life.

Sarah takes a polishing cloth to the surface of the mirror. "Must keep you tidy," she says.

"Are you coming?" she yells. "Steven, I said are you coming?" she repeats.

Steven jumps down from his high perch in the driver's seat. He joins Sarah at the back of the truck.

"Here, let me give you a hand lifting that into the truck." Steven takes hold of the top end of the mirror, while Sarah handles the foot. As the mirror is being loaded, Sarah finishes polishing the small brass nametag at the end of the mirror. A five, letter name is etched on its surface, it reads, KEVIN.

Sarah and Steven store the mirror along side the other fifty or so, name tagged mirrors. David, Jimmy, Mark and Alex are but a few of the visible names. They lock down the door and get into the cab of the truck. Steven turns and looks at the now familiar clown face of Mr. Trottier and cloaked image of his wife Zambora, in the rear seats of the truck. "So are we ready?" he asks them both.

Mr. Trottier smiles a wild toothy grin at Steven and nods his head in agreement. Steven accelerates the big rig.

Their truck pulled out to join up with the caravan, on its way to **your town.**

THE END

BOOK ONE

"Right this way, right this way, the exit is right this way. Step lively now, don't dawdle and be sure to come again. I do so hope that you enjoyed my little story. You can go to bed now and try to go to sleep, if you dare. Don't worry, the carnival isn't in your town yet, you can close your eyes to the safety of a dream. Do be sure to join me again next time. With the aid of my Dragon Stick, we will weave another tale of CHEAP CHILLS".

Proffessor T. LeeZard